SECRETS OF THE LIBRARY OF DOOM

DOOM SCHOOL

D1638116

BY MICHAEL DAHL
ILLUSTRATED BY PATRICIO CLAREY

Raintree is an imprint of Capstone Global Library Limited, a company
incorporated in England and Wales having its registered office at 264
Banbury Road, Oxford, OX2 7DY – Registered company number: 6695582

www.raintree.co.uk
myorders@raintree.co.uk

Text © Capstone Global Library Limited 2022
The moral rights of the proprietor have been asserted.

Designed by Hilary Wacholz
Original illustrations © Capstone Global Library Limited 2022
Originated by Capstone Global Library Ltd

978 1 3982 2359 2

British Library Cataloguing in Publication Data
A full catalogue record for this book is available from the British Library.

Printed and bound in India

CONTENTS

The Library of Doom is a hidden fortress.
It holds the world's largest collection
of strange and dangerous books.

Behold the Librarian. He defends the Library – and
the world – from super-villains, clever thieves
and fierce monsters. Many of his adventures
have remained secret. Now they can be told.

SECRET #880
WITH THE RIGHT BOOK,
FOES CAN BECOME FRIENDS.

Chapter One

INSIDE ICE

An iceberg **FLOATS** off the frozen coast of Antarctica.

It is a jagged mountain of blue and white ICE.

The largest part of all icebergs lies below the water. But this iceberg holds a **STRANGE** secret.

Deep in the watery depths GLOWS a yellow light.

The light shines from a **HUGE** window in the side of the iceberg.

Four figures stand by the window.

There are two girls. Their names are Wren and Ash.

The two boys are River and Stone.

They are training to become Pages of the **LIBRARY OF DOOM**. Pages help the Librarian with difficult jobs.

SSLLAAAAMMMMMM!

A metal cover **SLIDES** down over the window.

"No more standing around!" **SHOUTS** a tall figure.

It is the Trainer. "Follow me," he says.

The four young Pages follow the Trainer **DEEP** into the iceberg.

At the end of a long hall is a huge room. Shelves and books line the stone walls.

The Trainer **SPREADS** his arms.

"These books will teach you how to fight our enemies," he says. "Especially the Four Great Foes!"

Chapter Two

SHARK SIGN

Four **STRANGE** statues sit in the four corners of the room.

One is a two-headed shark. There is also a dragon, a mole and a vulture.

"It's the Four Foes!" says the boy Stone.

"And who can name the Four Foes?" asks the Trainer.

Wren says, *"The Four Great Foes all books beware: Water, Fire, Earth and Air."*

"This is FIRE," says Ash. She walks over to the dragon statue.

"This must be WATER," says River.

He pats the statue of the two-headed shark. Each head holds a METAL ball in its jaws.

But one of the shark heads drops its metal ball.

KLAANNNGGG!

The ball crashes to the floor and **ROLLS** towards Stone.

"Look out!" shouts the Trainer.

Stone **WAVES** his hand, and the
ball turns to dust.

The sound of the ball **HITTING** the floor still echoes in the room.

The Trainer turns to River and says, "The METAL balls are a sign."

"A sign of what?" asks Ash.

"Of danger," says the Trainer. "The balls only fall when a foe is nearby."

He points to River. "You must be an **ENEMY** in disguise!"

Chapter Three

HIDDEN FOE

River **SHAKES** his head. "No! It was an accident," he says.

"The statue never lies!" yells the Trainer.

The man waves his hand. Books **FLY** off the shelves.

They **SURROUND** River in the shape of a cage.

"He is still dangerous," warns Stone. "He can still use his powers."

Stone points to the cage of books.

ZZROOOOOOOSHHHH!

Pages wriggle out from the covers.

The pages **WRAP** tightly around River's body. They cover his mouth.

"There. Now he is unable to help," says Stone.

Wren blinks. "Help who?" she asks.

"You!" **SHOUTS** Stone.

The boy's Page uniform melts away. Underneath is a suit of bright red. His red hair shines in the light.

With a wave of the boy's hand, the others are **BLOWN** back by a gust of wind.

Ribbons slither out of books and tie each person to the shelves.

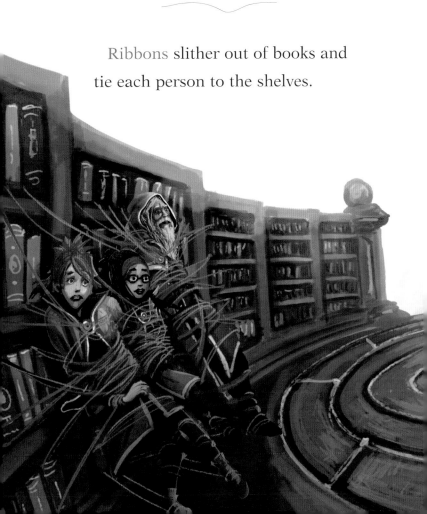

The Pages and their Trainer
are **TRAPPED**.

Chapter Four

RED PENCIL

The boy who was Stone stands in the middle of the room and laughs.

"Who are you?" **SHOUTS** the Trainer.

"I am Red Pencil," says the red-haired boy. "I've been training with FOLD, the Foes Opposing the Library of Doom."

"That shark statue was trying to warn us about *you*!" says Ash.

Red Pencil smiles. "This is my final assignment," he says. "**DESTROY** the training books of the Library!"

The boy villain holds up a large pencil with a **SHARP** point.

"With this, I can create or destroy," he says. "Today, I will destroy."

The boy kneels down. Using the pencil, he writes on the ground:

A HOLE IN THE FLOOR.

Suddenly, a large round **HOLE** appears in place of the writing.

"Water will **RISE** into the room," says Red Pencil. "Soon, these books will be useless."

Red Pencil stares at the **TRAPPED** Pages and Trainer.

"You will all be useless too," the boy villain says. "Frozen with your books."

WATER begins to cover the floor.

Chapter Five

FINAL FOUR

Red Pencil **TURNS** towards the door. "Time to say goodbye," he says.

Wren shouts out, "Good is always close by!"

Suddenly the EYES of the dragon statue glow. Flames shoot from its mouth.

The fire evaporates the cold water in the room.

Red Pencil looks at his prisoners. "Which one of you did that?" he yells.

The flames **SHOOT** out again.

This time a **DARK** shadow moves inside the flames.

"The Librarian!" gasps Red Pencil.

The Librarian steps out of the FLAMES.

He shouts a Word of Power.

The villain's pencil flies into the hero's hand.

The Librarian **WAVES** the pencil in a circle. The ribbons holding the Trainer and the two Pages disappear.

Then the statues come **ALIVE**.

The two-headed shark drops the other **METAL** ball. It rolls across the floor and plugs up the hole.

The Librarian commands the Earth Foe to dig into the book cage. The mole **RIPS** the pages wrapped around River.

All the Pages and their Trainer are now free.

Red Pencil turns to run away, but the Air Foe **SWOOPS** down. The vulture grabs the villain in its claws.

The three Pages clap and **CHEER**.

"I guess Red Pencil **FAILED** his assignment," says River.

The Librarian nods at Wren. "You're right," says the hero. "Good *is* always close by."

The Trainer **DUSTS** off his robe.

"Let's go, people," he says. "You can chat with the Librarian later. Our class is still in session!"

GLOSSARY

depth a place far below the surface

destroy to put an end to something

disguise a set of clothes and other things used to make a person look like someone or something else

evaporate to change from a liquid to a gas

foe an enemy

page a person who works for an important person, doing a variety of errands or jobs

session a period of time for a lesson or other activity

slither to move like a snake

statue a figure, usually in the shape of a human or animal, that is made from stone, metal or other materials

TALK ABOUT IT

1. Why do you think the Pages' secret school is in an iceberg? Why would this be a good place to have a school? How might it be a bad place?

2. How do you think the Pages felt when they learned their classmate Stone was actually an enemy in disguise? What makes you think that?

WRITE ABOUT IT

1. The Pages are young people who help the Librarian. If you could be a helper to any hero, who would it be? Why? What would you do? Write two paragraphs about your choice.

2. Imagine a new villain in the evil FOLD group. What are the villain's powers? What do they look like?

ABOUT THE AUTHOR

Michael Dahl is an award-winning author of more than 200 books for young people. He especially likes to write scary or weird fiction. His latest series are the sci-fi adventure Escape from Planet Alcatraz and School Bus of Horrors. As a child, Michael spent lots of time in libraries. "The creepier, the better," he says. These days, besides writing, he likes travelling and hunting for the one, true door that leads to the Library of Doom.

ABOUT THE ILLUSTRATOR

Patricio Clarey was born in Argentina. He graduated in fine arts from the Martín A. Malharro School of Visual Arts, specializing in illustration and graphic design. Patricio currently lives in Barcelona, Spain, where he works as a freelance graphic designer and illustrator. He has created several comics and graphic novels, and his work has been featured in books and other publications.